The Ch'i-lin Purse

THE
Ch'i-lin Purse

A Collection of Ancient Chinese Stories

RETOLD BY
LINDA FANG

PICTURES BY
JEANNE M. LEE

 HAMPTON-BROWN

Hampton-Brown
P.O. Box 223220
Carmel, California 93922
800-333-3510
www.hampton-brown.com

Printed in the United States of America

ISBN-13: 978-0-7362-3143-5
ISBN-10: 0-7362-3143-9

08 09 10 11 12 13 14 15 10 9 8 7 6 5 4

Contents

Introduction

The Ch'i-lin Purse is a collection of stories from ancient Chinese folklore. Folklore is the traditional beliefs and knowledge of a culture. Folklore includes stories, poems, songs, and drama. Almost every known society, or group of people, has created its own folklore.

Societies depend on **storytellers** to pass on their cultural beliefs and **morals**. People tell stories every day. But there is something different about true storytellers. Some storytellers are religious figures. Others are rulers or warriors. Some create music. Others create paintings or sculptures. They may add or delete details as they retell the culture's stories. This makes the stories grow and change over time.

Every culture's folklore is unique, but it is easy to find similarities between them. Some stories involve magical lands with fictional creatures. Many stories

Key Concepts

storyteller *n.* person who tells or performs stories or personal accounts of an event

moral *n.* conclusion about how to behave

involve animals, spirits, or enemies in **disguise**. Many cultures have stories about characters who play tricks on each other, or are searching for love. Characters often have to use their **intelligence** to fight an enemy or save someone's life. Battles with **authority** are often involved.

China has a long history of exciting folklore. Author Linda Fang grew up listening to folk tales from classic Chinese novels. In *The Ch'i-lin Purse*, Fang retells stories such as "The Ho-shih Jade" and "The Clever Magistrate" that come from these novels.

Fang also includes some of her favorite stories from Chinese opera. Opera is a form of musical drama. An opera is performed on a stage in front of an audience. There are over 300 forms of opera in China. These different types reflect the local interests of communities. Many Chinese opera singers use shrill, or high-pitched, voices. They wear colorful masks and costumes. The music is loud and involves many percussion instruments. "The Ch'i-lin Purse" and "The Two Miss Peonys" are two of the operas Fang retells as stories.

Key Concepts

disguise *n.* something worn to change a person's appearance
intelligence *n.* mental strength, such as cleverness or smartness
authority *n.* person or group with official power

The Ch'i-lin Purse has stories that include many different types of characters. All of these characters need help with their problems. Should they solve their problems alone, or should they ask for help from others?

Fang the Storyteller

Linda Fang has had a long career as a storyteller. Fang was shy as a child. When she was ten years old, Fang's teacher encouraged her to retell a story. Fang fell in love with storytelling. She has a unique way of capturing the audience's attention.

Fang has even competed in professional storytelling competitions. She has won many awards. These include the 2004 Solo Theatrical Performer, the 1998 Storyteller of the Year, and the 1996 Tellable Tale Award.

The Ch'i-lin Purse

It is said that many years ago in China, in a small town called Teng-chou, there lived a wealthy widow, Mrs. Hsüeh. She had only one daughter, Hsüeh Hsiang-ling. Hsiang-ling was beautiful and intelligent, and her mother loved her dearly. But since everything Hsiang-ling wanted was given to her, she became **rather spoiled**.

When Hsiang-ling was sixteen years old, her mother decided that it was time for her to marry. Through a **matchmaker**, Hsiang-ling was engaged to a young man from a wealthy family in a neighboring town.

Mrs. Hsüeh wanted to prepare a **dowry for Hsiang-ling that no girl in town could match**.

....

rather spoiled used to getting everything

matchmaker person who arranges marriages

dowry for Hsiang-ling that no girl in town could match
collection of money and belongings for Hsiang-ling's new
family that was better than anyone else's

But Hsiang-ling was hard to please. Almost everything her mother bought for her was returned or exchanged at least two or three times.

When the dowry was finally complete, Mrs. Hsüeh decided to add one more item to it. It was the Ch'i-lin Purse, a red satin bag **embroidered** on both sides with a *ch'i-lin*, a legendary animal from ancient times. The *ch'i-lin* had scales all over its body and a single horn on its head. In the old Chinese tradition, the *ch'i-lin* is the symbol of a **promising male offspring**. Mrs. Hsüeh wanted to give Hsiang-ling the purse because she hoped that her daughter would give birth to a talented son.

When the purse Mrs. Hsüeh had ordered was ready, a family servant brought it home. But Hsiang-ling was not satisfied at all. "I don't like the pattern, take it back!" she said.

The servant returned to the store and ordered another. But when it was brought home, Hsiang-ling **merely glanced at it** and said, "The colors of the *ch'i-lin* are too dark, take it back!"

The servant went to place another order, but the new purse still did not please her. This time the servant

---

embroidered that had a design sewn
promising male offspring good son
merely glanced at it only looked at it quickly

broke down in tears.

"I won't go back again, young mistress. The people in the store laugh at me. They say I am hard to please. This is not true. You are the one who is hard to please. If you don't want this purse, I am going to leave you and work for someone else."

Although Hsiang-ling was spoiled, she was not a **mean-spirited** person. She somehow began to feel sorry for the old man, who had been with her family for more than forty years. So she looked at the purse and said, "All right, I will have this one. You may go and pay for it." The servant went back to the store, paid for the purse, and gave it to Mrs. Hsüeh.

Hsiang-ling's wedding fell on the eighteenth day of the sixth month according to the lunar calendar. It was the day Hsiang-ling had **longed for** since her engagement. She was very excited and yet a bit sad, because she knew she was leaving her mother and the home she had lived in for sixteen years.

Hsiang-ling wore a red silk dress and a red silk veil over her head. As she sat in her *hua-chiao,* a **sedan chair draped** with red satin, and waited to be carried to her

....

broke down in tears started to cry
mean-spirited mean, rude
longed for waited for
sedan chair draped chair carried by servants covered

new home, her mother came to present her with the Ch'i-lin Purse.

"My dear child," she said as she lifted up the satin curtain in front, "this is your *ta-hsi-jih-tzu*, your big, happy day. I am delighted to see you get married even though I will miss you terribly. Here is the Ch'i-lin Purse. I have put some wonderful things in it. But don't open it now. Wait until you are in your new home, and you will feel that I am with you."

Hsiang-ling was hardly listening. She was thinking about the wedding and wondering about her husband-to-be, whom she had never met. She took the purse and laid it on her lap. A few minutes later, four **footmen** came. Picking up the *hua-chiao,* they placed it on their shoulders, and the wedding **procession** began.

As the procession reached the road, it started to rain. Soon it was pouring so heavily that the footmen could not see well enough to continue. The wedding procession **came to a halt**, and the *hua-chiao* was carried into a **pavilion** that stood alongside the road.

There was another *hua-chiao* in the pavilion. It was shabby, with holes in the drapes. Hsiang-ling could hear

....

footmen servants
procession parade, march
came to a halt stopped
pavilion tent

a girl sobbing inside. This annoyed her, because she believed that a person crying on her wedding day could bring bad luck. So she told her maid to go and find out what was wrong.

"The bride is very sad," the maid said when she returned. "She is poor and has nothing to take to her new home."

Hsiang-ling couldn't help feeling sorry for the girl. Then her eyes **fell on** the Ch'i-lin Purse in her lap. She realized that she was lucky to have so many things, while this girl had nothing. Since she wasn't carrying any money with her, she handed the Ch'i-lin Purse to her maid. "Give this to the girl, but don't mention my name."

So the maid went over and gave the purse to the other bride. The girl stopped crying **at once**. Hsiang-ling had given away her mother's wedding gift without ever finding out what was inside.

A few minutes later, the rain stopped, the footmen picked up Hsiang-ling's *hua-chiao,* and the procession **continued on its way**. In an hour, Hsiang-ling arrived at her new home. She was happily married that

....

fell on looked at

at once immediately

continued on its way began moving again

evening, and to her delight she **found her husband to be** a wonderful and handsome young man. In a year's time, when she became the mother of a little boy, she felt she was the happiest woman in the world.

But six years later, there came a terrible flood. Hsiang-ling and her family lost their home and everything they owned. When they were fleeing their town, Hsiang-ling became separated from her husband and young son in the crowds of other townspeople. After searching for them **in vain**, Hsiang-ling followed a group of people to another town called Lai-chou. She had given up hope that she would ever see her husband and child again.

As Hsiang-ling sat, exhausted and alone, at the side of the road leading to Lai-chou, a woman came up to her and said, "You must be hungry. Don't you know that a *li* down the road there is a **food-distribution shack**? Yüan-wai Lu has opened it to help the flood victims. Talk to his **butler**. I am sure you can get something to eat there."

Hsiang-ling thanked the woman, followed her directions, and found the place. A long line of people

....

found her husband to be discovered that her husband was
in vain without any success
food-distribution shack place to get free food
butler employee; personal helper

with bowls in their hands were waiting to get a **ration** of porridge. Hsiang-ling had never done such a thing in her life. As she stood in line holding a bowl and waiting her turn, she felt distraught enough to cry, but she forced herself to hold back the tears.

Finally, when it was her turn, Yüan-wai Lu's butler scooped the last portion of porridge into her bowl and said to the rest of the people in line, "Sorry, no more porridge left. Come back early tomorrow."

The person behind Hsiang-ling began to sob. Hsiang-ling turned around and saw a woman who reminded her of her mother, except that she was much older. Without **a word**, she emptied her porridge into the woman's bowl and walked away.

The butler was surprised at what Hsiang-ling had done. Just as she had made her way back to the road, he caught up with her and said, "Young lady, I don't understand. Why did you give away your porridge—are you not hungry?"

"I am hungry," said Hsiang-ling, "but I am young and I **can stand hunger a bit longer**."

"You are very unselfish," said the man. "I would

....

ration portion; small amount

a word saying anything

can stand hunger a bit longer do not need food as much as she does like to help you. My master, Yüan-wai Lu, is looking for someone to take care of his little boy. If you are interested, I would be happy to recommend you."

Hsiang-ling gratefully accepted his offer and was brought to the house where Yüan-wai Lu and his wife lived.

Yüan-wai Lu, a man in his early thirties, was impressed with Hsiang-ling's **graceful bearing**, and he agreed to hire her. "My wife's health is very **delicate** and she seldom leaves her room. Your job is to take care of our son. You may play with him anywhere in the garden, but there is one place you must never go. That is the Pearl Hall, the house that stands by itself on the east side of the garden. It is a sacred place, and if you ever go in there, you will **be dismissed** immediately."

So Hsiang-ling began her life as a **governess**. The little boy in her care was very spoiled. Whenever he wanted anything, he wanted it right away, and if he didn't get it, he would cry and cry until he got it. Hsiang-ling was saddened by his behavior; it reminded her of how spoiled she had been as a child.

One day, Hsiang-ling and the little boy were in

....

graceful bearing good behavior; politeness
delicate bad
be dismissed lose your job; be fired
governess caretaker, nanny

the garden. Suddenly, the ball they were playing with disappeared through the window of the Pearl Hall. The boy began to **wail**. "I want my ball, I want my ball! Go and get my ball!"

"Young Master, I cannot go into the Pearl Hall," said Hsiang-ling. "Your father doesn't allow it. I will be dismissed if I do."

But the little boy only cried louder, and finally Hsiang-ling decided that she had no choice. She walked over to the east side of the garden and looked around. **No one was in sight.** She quickly walked up the steps that led to the Pearl Hall and again made sure that no one was watching. Then she opened the door and stepped in.

She found herself standing in front of **an altar**, where two candles and some incense sticks were burning. But in the place where people usually **put the wooden name-tablets of** their ancestors was the Ch'i-lin Purse! Instantly she recalled the events of her wedding day and how happy she had been. She thought of her wonderful husband and her own son and how much she missed them. She had had everything then,

....

wail cry, whine

No one was in sight. She did not see anyone.

an altar a religious table

put the wooden name-tablets of honored

and now she had nothing! Hsiang-ling burst into tears.

Suddenly, she felt a hand on her shoulder. When she turned around she found herself face-to-face with Mrs. Lu, her mistress, and a young maid.

"What are you doing here?" Mrs. Lu asked angrily.

"Young Master told me to come here and pick up his ball," Hsiang-ling replied.

"Then why were you weeping at the altar?"

"Because I saw the purse that once belonged to me."

Mrs. Lu looked startled. "Where are you from?" she asked, as she took the purse from the altar and sat down on a chair that leaned against a long table. **There was a tremble in her voice.**

"I am from Teng-chou."

"Bring her a stool," said Mrs. Lu, motioning to her maid. Not wanting to **wait on** another servant, the maid **grudgingly** brought a stool and put it to Mrs. Lu's right. "You may sit down," said Mrs. Lu. Somewhat confused, Hsiang-ling sat down.

"What was your **maiden name**?"

"Hsüeh Hsiang-ling."

"When were you married?"

....

There was a tremble in her voice. She sounded nervous.

wait on serve, help

grudgingly angrily, stubbornly

maiden name full name before you were married

"On the eighteenth day of the sixth moon, six years ago."

"Bring her a chair and put it to my left," Mrs. Lu ordered her maid. Hsiang-ling was told to move to the chair. She was surprised to see herself treated as a guest of honor.

"Tell me how you lost the purse," said Mrs. Lu.

"It was a gift from my mother. My wedding procession was stopped on the road because of a storm, and my *hua-chiao* was carried into a pavilion. There was another *hua-chiao* in it, and the bride was crying."

"Move her chair to the middle and move mine to the right side," ordered Mrs. Lu. The chairs were switched, and once again Hsiang-ling was told to sit down. She was **astonished** to find herself sitting in the middle seat—the place of the highest honor.

"Please continue," said Mrs. Lu.

"I gave the bride my purse. I never saw it again, and I have no idea how it got here."

Mrs. Lu **dropped to** her knees in front of Hsiang-ling and cried, "You are **my benefactor**! All these years I have been praying here for your well-being.

---

astonished very surprised

dropped to got down on

my benefactor the person who helped me

When I got to my new home, I opened the purse and found it full of valuables, including this." She opened the purse and took out a piece of jade. "My husband and I were able to **pawn** it for a large amount of money. Using the money, we started a business and have now become very wealthy. So I **reclaimed** the jade and have kept it in the purse since. We also built the Pearl Hall to house the purse and to honor you.

"I knew that you lived in the Teng-chou area, so when I heard about the flood I prayed day and night in that direction, begging Buddha to protect you from harm. I was hoping that one day I would find you and **show you my gratitude**. And here you are, taking care of my son! I know what we must do. We shall divide our property and give you half of it. That will make us all very happy."

Hsiang-ling was **speechless** as Mrs. Lu placed the purse in her hands. That same day, Yüan-wai Lu sent out servants in all directions to look for Hsiang-ling's husband and son. Soon they were found, in a village not far from Teng-chou.

A great friendship developed between the two

....

pawn sell

reclaimed bought back

show you my gratitude thank you

speechless so happy that she could not speak

families. Later, whenever Hsiang-ling told people the story about her purse, she would always end the tale by saying, "If you have a chance to do something good, be sure to do it. **Happiness will come back to you.**"

....

Happiness will come back to you. You will be rewarded.

BEFORE YOU MOVE ON...

1. **Character** Reread pages 15–17. Hsiang-ling is a beautiful young woman. What else do you know about her?

2. **Cause and Effect** Reread pages 23–24. Why does Mrs. Lu give Hsiang-ling the middle seat of honor?

The Two Miss Peonys

It is said that some nine hundred years ago, during the Northern Sung Dynasty, there lived a young man named Chang Chen. When Chang Chen was still a boy, he was engaged to a beautiful and wealthy girl about his own age through matchmaking. Her name was Miss Chin Peony. Unfortunately, some years later, Chang Chen's parents died and left him with very little money. Hoping to get some **support**, he traveled all the way to the capital, Pien-liang, where **his betrothed** and her parents lived.

What Chang Chen didn't know was that Miss Peony's father, Mr. Chin, **a high official in the capital, was very snobbish**. Mr. Chin didn't want his

----

support money or help

his betrothed the girl he was supposed to marry

a high official in the capital, was very snobbish an important man in the city, was very rude daughter to marry a poor man and planned to break the engagement. But since he did not have an excuse to do so, he **received Chang Chen coldly and put him up** in a study located in a **remote** corner of the garden. "You should prepare for the imperial examinations," he said. "Until you pass them and become a high official in the court, I will not allow you to marry my daughter."

Chang Chen never had a chance to see Miss Peony. He tried his best to study during the day, and often in the evening he would stand by the pond in the garden and watch a carp-fish swimming. One evening as he stood there he sighed and said, "Oh, carp-fish, how free and happy you are! And yet I know you are as lonely as I am. We have only each other for company."

Now, the carp-fish was actually a spirit. She **empathized with** Chang Chen and wanted to console him. So one evening, while Chang Chen was studying, she leaped out of the water, struck the ground with her tail three times, and turned herself into a girl who looked exactly like Miss Chin Peony.

The carp-fish spirit walked into Chang Chen's study and found him dozing at his desk. She took some water

....

received Chang Chen coldly and put him up was mean to Chang Chen and made him stay

remote faraway

empathized with felt sorry for

from his cup and sprinkled it on the young man's face.

Chang Chen woke up at once. He was surprised to see a beautiful girl in his study. "Who are you?" he asked. "Why are you here?"

"I am your **betrothed**, Miss Chin Peony," said the carp-fish spirit. "I knew you were here, and wanted to visit."

Chang Chen was delighted to hear this. He quickly stood up and, making a deep bow, invited her to sit down. "I am so happy you have come. It is wonderful to finally meet you."

"I had to come at night," said the carp-fish spirit. "My father **forbids** me to see you. He wanted to **call off** our engagement, but I begged him not to. I hope you'll pass the examinations. Then my father will allow us to marry."

Chang Chen **was deeply touched**. "I promise you, I will try hard not to disappoint you. May I hope to see you again?"

"Tomorrow after sunset, wait for me near the pond," said the carp-fish spirit. "I will meet you there."

From then on, the two met at the pond every

....

betrothed fiancé; future wife
forbids will not allow
call off end
was deeply touched felt very happy

evening. Chang Chen never suspected that the girl was in fact a spirit.

Soon the fifteenth day of the new year arrived. It was the Yüan-hsiao Festival—the Festival of Lanterns. Miss Peony and her parents went into the garden to enjoy the evening. The carp-fish spirit, who had been waiting for Chang Chen by the pond, quickly hid herself behind a willow tree, for fear of being caught as **an impostor**. Chang Chen, arriving there a few minutes late, saw Miss Peony and went over to talk to her.

Now, Miss Peony had never met Chang Chen before. When she saw him, she began to scream: "**Bandit**, bandit, help, help!"

Her father was furious when he saw Chang Chen. "How dare you approach my daughter," he **blasted**. "Get out of here!" He ordered his servants to throw Chang Chen out of the garden.

Chang Chen was deeply hurt. The carp-fish spirit caught up with him outside the **estate** and began to walk with him. But Chang Chen thought she was the girl who had called him a bandit, and he refused to

....

an imposter a fake; someone in disguise as Miss Peony

Bandit Thief

blasted yelled, screamed

estate family home

talk to her.

"I had to pretend that I didn't know you," explained the carp-fish spirit, "otherwise my father would have punished me for talking to you. I think the best thing for us to do is to leave this place and get married."

"I am very poor," said Chang Chen. "If you marry me, you will have to live a hard life."

"I have some money with me," said the carp-fish spirit. "Besides, we can always find ways to **make a living**. Don't you worry."

Chang Chen finally believed the girl was telling him the truth and agreed to do as she had suggested. The two decided to leave the capital at once.

As they walked through the streets, they found that the Yüan-hsiao festivities had already begun. Firecrackers were **going off** everywhere. The streets were crowded. A parade of colorful lanterns **resembling** different kinds of animals and historical figures moved on as the crowds watched and cheered.

Unfortunately for the young lovers, Miss Peony's father, Mr. Chin, together with several other high officials, had come to watch the celebration. From the

....

make a living earn money
going off exploding
resembling that looked like

platform on which he was standing, he saw Chang Chen and the carp-fish spirit in the crowd. Thinking his daughter had run away with Chang Chen, Mr. Chin **flew into a rage**. His guards were ordered to arrest the couple and take them back to his house.

The moment Mr. Chin returned home he began to yell at his wife: "How dare you let our daughter run away with this **penniless man and disgrace us**!"

"*Lao-yeh,* you are wrong," said his wife. "Our daughter never **set foot out of** the house. She is in her chamber. I can get her right away."

Mr. Chin's eyes were as large as walnuts when he saw his daughter appear in the doorway with his wife. "Then who was the girl we caught running away with Chang Chen? Bring them both in!" he commanded his guards.

Mr. Chin could not believe his eyes. In front of him stood two Miss Peonys!

The real Miss Peony was very angry. "Who are you?" she said to the carp-fish spirit. "How dare you **impersonate** me!"

---

flew into a rage got very angry

penniless man and disgrace us poor man and embarrass us

set foot out of left

impersonate pretend to be

The carp-fish spirit realized that she had to go along with the story she had made up for Chang Chen, so she said, "I *am* Miss Peony. You are the impostor!"

The two began to quarrel, each accusing the other of being the impostor. Mr. Chin was totally confused. He finally decided to contact Pao Kung, the **imperial investigator**, for help.

When the carp-fish spirit heard this, she began to worry. Since Pao Kung had the power to **expel demons** and spirits, she would be forced to reveal her identity.

Late at night, when nobody was watching, the carp-fish spirit hurried back to the pond. "Tortoise spirit!" she called. "I am in great danger!"

The tortoise spirit emerged from the water. "What is it, my dear carp-fish? What's wrong?"

"Mr. Chin has sent for Pao Kung. If he comes tomorrow, he will force me to reveal my true identity. I will then have to leave Chang Chen."

"Don't you worry," said the tortoise spirit. "I will deal with Pao Kung."

The next morning, the tortoise spirit turned himself

....

imperial investigator person who investigates crime
expel demons force out evil ghosts

into Pao Kung, changed his little shrimp and crab friends into guards, and formed an instant procession. They went out through the back entrance of the garden and onto the road. **Having gone a distance**, they turned around and marched back toward the mansion. Just before they reached it, the tortoise-spirit Pao Kung saw the real Pao Kung and his guards coming from the opposite direction.

Mr. Chin was **flabbergasted** when he saw the two processions—two Pao Kungs, each escorted by their guards. "Oh, what am I going to do?" he cried. But he had to allow them both into his house, since he could not determine who was truly Pao Kung.

The real Pao Kung was **outraged** to see someone impersonating him. He ordered his guards to bring him his sword, which had the **supernatural** power to expose the original shapes of spirits.

"Wait," cried the tortoise spirit as the real Pao Kung raised his sword. "Pao Kung is wise and just. If you are the real Pao Kung, try to solve this case with fairness. If you cannot, you are no Pao Kung."

Pao Kung agreed and put down his sword. Two

....

Having gone a distance After they had walked for a while
flabbergasted confused, surprised
outraged shocked and angry
supernatural magical

temporary courts were set up in the hall. The real Pao Kung sat at a desk on the left side; the tortoise-spirit Pao Kung sat at a desk on the right side.

"**Open court!**" said the real Pao Kung.

"Open court!" imitated the tortoise spirit.

"*Ouh! . . . Ouh! . . . Ouh!*" cried the guards of the real Pao Kung.

"*Ouh! . . . Ouh! . . . Ouh!*" imitated the shrimp and crab soldiers with delight.

The two Pao Kungs ordered the two Miss Peonys and Chang Chen to be brought in.

Still quarreling with each other, the girls entered. Then they took turns telling their stories. Each **insisted** that she was the real Miss Peony who had lived in her father's house all her life.

The real Pao Kung was **soon convinced** which of the two was the real Miss Peony, but he **sympathized with** the carp-fish spirit and admired her for her love for Chang Chen. He decided not to reveal her identity, because he knew that it would mean an end to her relationship with the young man.

Shaking his head and pretending that he could not

Open court! We will hear the evidence now!

insisted claimed

soon convinced quickly certain he knew

sympathized with felt sorry for

tell the difference, he said, "I cannot solve this case. It is giving me a headache. I am going home." He rose and left with his guards.

The tortoise-spirit Pao Kung, laughing to himself, also left with his shrimp and crab soldiers.

Mr. Chin was very upset. "I am going to **appeal** to the Jade Emperor and request that he send Chang T'ien-shih, the **Sorcerer from Heaven**, to expel the evil spirit."

The carp-fish spirit knew that Chang T'ien-shih was **merciless**, so she decided to tell Chang Chen the truth. Taking him aside, she said, "I am only a carp-fish spirit. I love you and impersonated your betrothed. Now I must go."

"Let's go together," said Chang Chen. "I don't love Miss Peony. All she cares about is herself. I want to marry you."

So the two walked out of Mr. Chin's house together.

Suddenly, they heard a voice from the sky. It was Chang T'ien-shih standing on a cloud flying toward them.

"Stop," cried Chang T'ien-shih. "I have come to

....

appeal write
Sorcerer from Heaven Magical Ruler from the Sky
merciless mean, unforgiving

conquer the evil spirit that dares to create chaos on
the earth!"

The two lovers ran as fast as they could, but Chang
T'ien-shih was quicker.

Finally, the carp-fish spirit **gave up hope**. She
threw herself on the ground and began to weep. Just
then she heard a gentle voice calling her.

"Carp-fish spirit! Carp-fish spirit!"

When she looked up, she saw Kuan-yin, the Buddha
of **Compassion**, standing before her. "Oh, Kuan-yin,"
she cried, "please save me."

"Carp-fish spirit, listen to me," said Kuan-yin, as she
motioned Chang T'ien-shih to **withdraw**. "The world
is full of sorrow. A spirit is not allowed to mix with
human beings. Come with me and nurture yourself
with prayers and fasting, and you will become **an
immortal** someday."

"No," said the carp-fish spirit. "I love Chang
Chen. I want to marry him. Please make me a real
woman instead."

"Are you willing to give up your supernatural
power?" asked Kuan-yin.

....

gave up hope realized she could not win the battle
Compassion Kindness, Caring
withdraw not hurt the carp-fish
an immortal a being that can never die

"Yes, as long as I can marry Chang Chen," said the carp-fish spirit.

"**Think again**," said Kuan-yin. "You have nurtured your supernatural spirit for almost a thousand years, and you will soon become immortal. If you give up your power, you will only live a human life. You might regret your decision."

"No," said the carp-fish spirit. "I will never regret it."

"Very well," said Kuan-yin. "I will pluck out your three magic scales, and then you will become an ordinary woman. I'm afraid it is going to hurt **a great deal**." She waved her hand, and the spirit turned back into a carp-fish.

The carp-fish spirit felt terrible pain as Kuan-yin plucked out her three magic scales. She **somersaulted** three times. Immediately, all her supernatural power left her, and she became a real woman, far more beautiful than Miss Peony.

She ran back to the pond to say goodbye to her friends and then followed Chang Chen back to his hometown. They started to **build** a happy life, and

....

Think again Think seriously about your decision
a great deal a lot
somersaulted turned
build create

when they got married, all the shrimps, fish, and tortoises from the pond, as well as those from the lakes and seas, attended the wedding.

BEFORE YOU MOVE ON...

1. **Comparisons** One of the Miss Peonys is a spirit. What other ways are the two women different? Reread pages 30–31 and 36.

2. **Inference** Reread page 39. Why does Kuan-yin think the carp-fish spirit may regret becoming human?

The Ho-shih Jade

During the period of the Warring States, the kings of China made war on one another, fighting for power and land. When tired of fighting, they would send **envoys to negotiate a settlement**. These negotiations were sometimes called tongue wars. At one time, there were seven states: Ch'in, Ch'u, Ch'i, Yen, Han, Wei, and Chao. Ch'in was the strongest, while Chao was the weakest.

The king of Chao had a **chamberlain** named Miao Hsien. One day Miao Hsien bought a jadestone from a stranger for five hundred *liang* of gold. When he asked a jade expert to **appraise it**, he was told that it was the famous Ho-shih Jade, named after Pien Ho,

....

envoys to negotiate a settlement people to solve the problem

chamberlain man who took care of his house and employees

appraise it tell him how much it was worth

the man who discovered it. This jade was the rarest kind of precious stone in the world. In the dark, it **was luminous**; indoors, it would keep a room warm in winter and cool in summer and repel insects. The jade expert advised Miao Hsien to keep the jade in a safe place so that it would not be stolen.

The king of Chao somehow heard about the jade and asked Miao Hsien to show it to him. Miao Hsien feared that once the king saw the jade he would want it, so he planned to take the jade and run away. But one of Miao Hsien's houseguests, a man named Lin Hsiang-ju, advised him not to do so, saying that he would be asking for trouble. He persuaded Miao Hsien to offer the jade to the king as **a national treasure**.

Miao Hsien followed this advice; the king was delighted and **promoted Miao Hsien to a very high position**. Miao Hsien then realized that Lin Hsiang-ju had been very wise, so he entrusted him with other important matters.

Some time later, when the jade expert went to the state of Ch'in to set some jadestones, he told the king of Ch'in about the Ho-shih Jade and its unique features.

....

was luminous glowed
a national treasure something everyone could enjoy
promoted Miao Hsien to a very high position gave a more important job to Miao Hsien

The king of Ch'in, who was a very **ambitious** and greedy man, wanted the jade for himself. He gathered his officials and asked them how he could take the jade away from the state of Chao. His uncle and prime minister, Wei Jan, suggested that he offer fifteen cities in the Yu-yang area in exchange for the jade.

"What?" cried the king of Ch'in. "Is such a jade worth fifteen cities? Only a fool would do that."

"We would not be making the offer **in earnest**," said Wei Jan. "The king of Chao has always been afraid of us, because he fears that we are going to **invade his state**. Therefore, if we offer to exchange fifteen cities for the jade, he would not dare refuse. Once the jade is here, we can keep it. We will not give him the fifteen cities. Would he dare to ask for them?"

The king of Ch'in thought this was a good idea, so he sent an envoy to the king of Chao with a letter offering fifteen cities in the Yu-yang area for the jade.

As expected, this offer worried the king of Chao. He knew that if he sent the jade to the king of Ch'in he would not get the fifteen cities **in return**, and yet he did not dare refuse the offer, for fear that the king

···

ambitious determined

in earnest seriously

invade his state take his land

in return as an exchange

of Ch'in would declare war on the state of Chao. So he **summoned his high officials to court**.

The high officials offered all kinds of advice, but they could not agree on anything. One official then suggested that the king send a wise and brave man to the state of Ch'in as his envoy. If the king of Ch'in really **signed over the deeds of** the fifteen cities to Chao, the envoy should leave the jade there. If not, he should bring the jade back.

The king of Chao liked the idea, but he didn't know whom to send. He looked from one official to another, but they all lowered their heads and did not say a word.

Then Miao Hsien stepped forward and said, "I have a houseguest, Lin Hsiang-ju. He is both wise and brave. If *Ta-wang* appoints him envoy, I am sure he will be able to **accomplish the task successfully**."

So the king of Chao summoned Lin Hsiang-ju to the palace. He was delighted to find Lin Hsiang-ju an unusually intelligent man, but to make sure that he was capable of undertaking the task, the king asked, "The king of Ch'in has offered to exchange fifteen cities for the Ho-shih Jade; do you think that I should accept his offer?"

"Ch'in is strong and Chao is weak," said Lin Hsiang-ju. "It would not be wise for *Ta-wang* to turn down the offer."

"If the king of Ch'in takes the jade but does not give us the cities, what should we do?" asked the king of Chao, **testing him further**.

"The king of Ch'in is offering a high price for the jade," said Lin Hsiang-ju. "If we do not accept the offer, it will make us look very bad. If we present the jade to the king of Ch'in before he gives us fifteen cities, it will show that we are **sincere and courteous**. If the king of Ch'in denies us the fifteen cities when he has the jade in his hand, he will be in the wrong!" Lin Hsiang-ju paused, waiting to see the king's reaction.

"I plan to send an envoy to the state of Ch'in with the jade. Whom do you think I should send?" asked the king of Chao.

"I would be honored to go. If the king of Ch'in signs over to us the fifteen cities, I will leave the jade with him. **Otherwise, your lowly servant** will bring the jade safely back to *Ta-wang*," Lin Hsiang-ju replied

....

testing him further to see how smart Lin Hsiang-ju was
sincere and courteous honest and polite
Otherwise, your lowly servant If not, I

with confidence.

The king of Chao was pleased and appointed Lin Hsiang-ju his envoy. Lin Hsiang-ju then **laid out his plan in detail**.

After several days of preparation, including a five-day **fast and a solemn** farewell ceremony, Lin Hsiang-ju took the Ho-shih Jade and set out for Hsien-yang, the capital of Ch'in, accompanied only by a guard.

When the king of Ch'in heard that the envoy from Chao was coming with the jade, he was overjoyed. Seated **on his throne and flanked** by his officials, he summoned Lin Hsiang-ju to the palace as soon as he arrived.

With his head bowed, Lin Hsiang-ju approached the throne carrying a box that held the jade. He opened the box, took out the silk pouch that protected the jade, and offered it to the king of Ch'in.

The king opened the pouch and carefully removed its contents. **Immaculate, the stone gleamed** in his hands. It was truly a rare treasure. After examining the jade, the king passed it on to his officials, who

....

laid out his plan in detail told the King his whole plan
fast and a solemn time without food and a serious
on his throne and flanked in his royal chair and surrounded
Immaculate, the stone gleamed Perfect, the stone shone

immediately congratulated him for securing such a priceless gem. They shouted, "May *Ta-wang* live ten thousand years!"

The king of Ch'in then ordered his servant to take the jade to his wives and concubines and show it to them. Lin Hsiang-ju waited for a long time, but the jade was not returned to the king's table.

Seeing that the king mentioned nothing about the fifteen cities, Lin Hsiang-ju said, "There is a **flaw** in the jade. Please allow me to show it to *Ta-wang*."

The king quickly ordered his servant to bring the jade back to Lin Hsiang-ju. Once the jade was in Lin Hsiang-ju's hands, he took several steps backward until he was very close to a **pillar**. Then he said angrily to the king, "This jade is one of the most precious treasures in the world. *Ta-wang* wrote to the king of Chao offering fifteen cities for the jade. His Majesty discussed the proposal with his officials, who felt it might be a **ploy and tried to dissuade** him from accepting the offer. But I argued that because *Ta-wang* is such a powerful king, there is no reason to **doubt his sincerity**. My king followed my advice and sent

....

flaw mistake, problem, imperfection
pillar large stone structure
ploy and tried to dissuade trick and tried to stop
doubt his sincerity not trust him

me here with the jade. This shows how sincere he is. **On the other hand**, when *Ta-wang* took the jade from my hands, he did not even rise from his throne. Then *Ta-wang* showed the jade not only to his **subjects** but also to his wives and concubines. This is an insult to the precious jade. In addition, *Ta-wang* never mentioned the fifteen cities he had previously promised. It proves that *Ta-wang* has no **real intention** of exchanging fifteen cities for the jade. I am going to take the jade back to my king."

The bold Lin Hsiang-ju then pointed to the pillar. "If *Ta-wang* tries to take the jade from me by force, I will smash it and then my head on this pillar. We will both be destroyed, but *Ta-wang* will not get the jade either!" He raised the jade as if ready to **carry out his threat**.

"Don't do it!" cried the king of Ch'in. "I won't fail your king." He ordered one of his officials to bring a map. The map was placed on the table, and the king of Ch'in pointed out fifteen cities to Lin Hsiang-ju.

Suspecting the king of playing another trick, Lin Hsiang-ju said to him, "In order to please *Ta-wang*, His

....

On the other hand But, However
subjects employees
real intention plan
carry out his threat destroy the jade and himself

Majesty the king of Chao was willing to **relinquish** the jade. Before I left, he fasted for five days and summoned all his officials to see the jade off in a solemn ceremony. *Ta-wang* should follow his example: fast for five days, and receive the jade in a ceremony where envoys from other states are present. If *Ta-wang* refuses, I would rather die than **turn over** the jade to *Ta-wang*."

Seeing how determined Lin Hsiang-ju was, the king of Ch'in thought that it would be best to **go along with** his demands. He ordered a fast for five days and sent Lin Hsiang-ju back to his **lodgings**.

But Lin Hsiang-ju was afraid that the king of Ch'in might still have other tricks to play, so he ordered his guard to disguise himself as a poor man, tie the bag that contained the jade around his waist, and return to Chao. He also wrote a letter to the king of Chao saying that he was sending his guard back with the jade, while he himself was staying behind to deal with the king of Ch'in.

The king of Ch'in did not fast at all. He ordered his servants to decorate the palace and prepare many expensive gifts. Envoys from every state were invited to

---

relinquish give you
turn over give
go along with agree to
lodgings room

witness the ceremony.

When they had all arrived, the king of Ch'in summoned his official of **protocol to escort** Lin Hsiang-ju to the throne room. Lin Hsiang-ju walked up to the king and bowed. Seeing that Lin Hsiang-ju **was empty-handed**, the king said. "I have fasted for five days and am ready to receive the jade—where is it?"

Lin Hsiang-ju replied, "Since King Mu's reign, there have been twenty kings in the state of Ch'in, and all were **treacherous** and dishonest. *Ta-wang* has a similar reputation. For fear of being cheated and unable to fulfill my king's task, I ordered my guard to take the jade back to my king. For this I deserve death; please do with me whatever *Ta-wang* pleases." He bent his head and waited.

The king of Ch'in was furious. "You blamed me for not showing enough respect for the jade. I followed your advice and **met your demands**. And yet you sent the jade back to Chao. You have cheated me! I am going to kill you!" He ordered his guards to bind Lin Hsiang-ju with ropes.

Lin Hsiang-ju did not resist. "*Ta-wang* should listen

....

protocol to escort ceremonies to bring
was empty-handed did not have the jade
treacherous disloyal, mean
met your demands did what you wanted

to what I have to say; if **my words do not satisfy him**, it will not be too late to kill me."

"Speak!" said the king of Ch'in impatiently.

"Ch'in is strong and Chao is weak. The state of Chao cannot afford to make an enemy of the state of Ch'in. If *Ta-wang* really wants to exchange fifteen cities for the jade, why not send an envoy with me to Chao with the deed to the cities? When our king has the deed in his hands, he would not dare to keep the jade from *Ta-wang*. I know that I have offended *Ta-wang* and deserve death, so I have already informed my king that I may not return alive. *Ta-wang* **might as well throw me into a caldron of boiling oil**, so that all the kings will know that *Ta-wang* killed the envoy of Chao in his effort to possess the Ho–shih Jade. Let them decide who is right and who is wrong."

The king of Ch'in and his officials looked at one another without a word. All the envoys from the other states knew how cruel a man the king of Ch'in was, and **feared for Lin Hsiang-ju's life**.

Wei Jan, the king's uncle, quickly walked up to his nephew and whispered in his ear, "I don't think it is

....

my words do not satisfy him you do not like what I say

might as well throw me into a caldron of boiling oil should kill me

feared for Lin Hsiang-ju's life worried he would kill Lin Hsiang-ju wise to kill Lin Hsiang-ju now. It will not only ruin our reputation but also make the state of Chao our enemy. It would be better to let him go."

The king **nodded his head**. As the soldiers started to take Lin Hsiang-ju away, the king began to laugh. "Wait!" he said as he turned to Lin Hsiang-ju. "I was only testing your courage. I wanted to see what kind of person you really are and how you would react **in the face of death**. It seems to me now that you are really a brave man. The king of Chao is lucky to have you as his envoy. No, I am not going to kill you."

So instead of executing Lin Hsiang-ju, the king entertained him with a banquet and sent him back home. The king of Chao was so pleased with Lin Hsiang-ju's courage and ingenuity that he appointed him one of his highest-ranking officials.

The king of Ch'in never gave the king of Chao the fifteen cities he had promised. So, of course, he never got the jade.

....

nodded his head made a sign to kill Lin Hsiang-ju

in the face of death if you thought I would kill you

BEFORE YOU MOVE ON...

1. **Plot** Reread page 43. How does the king of Ch'in plan to trick the king of Chao?

2. **Conclusions** Reread pages 52–53. Lin Hsiang-ju tricks the king of Ch'in. Why doesn't the king kill him?

The Clever Magistrate

One cold winter day, a farmer was carrying two buckets of **spoiled** food from a restaurant to **his pigsty**. As he was passing a coat shop, he accidentally spilled some of the slop on the ground. Sour cabbage, rotten eggs, and fish bones scattered all over the ground. Ugh! Ugh! **What a smell!**

The shopkeeper, who happened to be standing inside the door, saw this and was furious. He rushed out, grabbed the man, and shouted, "You dirty **beggar**! Look what you've done in front of my shop! It will be impossible to get rid of the smell! How are you going to pay for the damage?"

"I am so sorry," said the farmer. "I will clean it up

---

spoiled rotten
his pigsty feed to his pigs
What a smell! It smelled terrible!
beggar poor person

right away. As for the damage, all I have is this coin."
He took out a coin and handed it to the shopkeeper.

The shopkeeper snatched the coin, put it between
his teeth, and bit down on it. The metal was soft, which
proved that it **contained silver**. He thrust it into his
pocket and said, "All right, I will take it. But you still
need to clean up the mess."

"Let me go and get some rags and a mop," said the
farmer. "I will be right back."

"No," said the shopkeeper. "I want you to clean it up
right away. It smells so bad that I am going to be sick.
Take off your coat and wipe up the mess."

"Please don't ask me to do that!" cried the farmer.
"This is the only quilted coat I have, and if I use it to
wipe up the mess, it will be ruined. I won't be able to
wear it anymore."

"That's your problem, not mine!" said the
shopkeeper. "In fact, the coat you are wearing is no
better than rags. If you don't do what I say, I am going
to take you to court."

The farmer **pleaded with him to reconsider**, but
the shopkeeper would not **relent**.

....

contained silver was a real coin; was worth something
pleaded with him to reconsider begged him not to
relent change his decision

Just then they heard, "**Make way for the magistrate!** Make way for the magistrate!"

The county magistrate was coming down the road in his sedan chair. When he saw the **commotion**, he ordered his guards to put down the chair and bring the two men before him.

"What is the matter?" he asked.

The shopkeeper quickly replied, "*Ta-jen*, this man made a mess in front of my shop. He gave me a coin to pay for the damage, but when I asked him to wipe up the mess, he wouldn't do it."

The magistrate stepped down from his chair and went over to look at the mess. Sour cabbage, rotten eggs, and fish bones were **scattered all over the place**. Ugh! Ugh! What a smell!

"Why don't you clean up the mess?" asked the magistrate.

"He wants me to wipe up the mess with my coat," said the farmer. "It will be ruined if I do so. And this is the only coat I have."

"Is that what you want?" the magistrate asked the shopkeeper.

....

Make way for the magistrate! Here comes the judge!
commotion argument
scattered all over the place everywhere

"Yes, that is exactly what I want."

"And you will not **settle for less**?"

"No, I will not settle for anything less."

"Well," said the magistrate to the farmer, "if that is what he wants, you'd better do it."

"*Ta-jen,* **have mercy**! I can't do that!" cried the farmer. "Without the coat I will freeze to death."

"I am sorry," said the magistrate. "But that doesn't change anything. If you don't do it, I will have to put you in jail."

"That is not just!" cried the farmer.

"Hmm . . ." said the magistrate. He looked angry.

"Ouh! Ouh! Ouh!" cried the guards. *"Ouh! Ouh! Ouh!"* They looked threatening.

The farmer realized that there was **no way out**. Reluctantly, he used his coat to clean up the mess. Sour cabbage, rotten eggs, and fish bones. Ugh! Ugh! What a smell! He threw the coat into one of his buckets and stood **shivering** in front of the magistrate.

The shopkeeper laughed. "Ha, ha, ha!"

"Well," said the magistrate to the shopkeeper, "are you satisfied now?"

....

settle for less agree to some other form of payment

have mercy please help me

no way out no way to keep his coat

shivering shaking because he was so cold

"Yes, *Ta-jen*, I am completely satisfied."

"No more complaints?"

"No more complaints!" said the shopkeeper.

"**Case closed**," said the magistrate.

"Case closed."

"But his case against you is now open."

"What!" said the shopkeeper, stunned.

"Well, you see, he is now freezing without a coat. In such weather he could catch a cold. Is that not possible?" asked the magistrate.

"Yes, *Ta-jen*."

"His cold could develop into **pneumonia**. Is that not possible?"

"Yes, *Ta-jen*."

"Then he could die. His family could **sue you** for murder, and if you are convicted, you would be put to death. Isn't that almost **inevitable**?"

"Yes, *Ta-jen*."

"Well, I don't think you can afford that, can you?"

"Oh, no, *Ta-jen*. I cannot afford that. What shall I do?"

"Well, it would be better to settle this out of court."

....

Case closed This problem has been solved
pneumonia a serious illness
sue you take you to court; blame you
inevitable certain

"Yes, yes, we'd better settle this out of court. But how?"

"We should get him a coat so he won't catch a cold."

"But where can we get one?"

"Right here, from your coat shop."

The shopkeeper looked **as if he had swallowed a fly alive**. He yelled at the farmer, "Go get a coat and be gone!"

The farmer went into the shop, picked out a very **cheap** coat, and came out. The magistrate stopped him.

"You poor thing!" he said. "Look at the coat you've got. It is so thin. You could still catch a cold, isn't that so?"

"Yes, *Ta-jen*."

"You might get pneumonia, isn't that so?"

"Yes, *Ta-jen*."

"You might even die, isn't that so?"

"Yes, *Ta-jen*."

"And then your family could come and **harass** this nice gentleman. I know all your tricks!" The magistrate turned to one of his guards. "Go into the shop and get him the warmest coat you can find."

---

as if he had swallowed a fly alive very surprised

cheap inexpensive

harass bother

So the guard went into the shop and picked out the warmest coat he could find for the farmer. As you might guess, the warmest coat happened to be the most expensive.

When the farmer left, the magistrate smiled at the shopkeeper. "Well, what do you think about the way I settled this case? Didn't I handle it very well?"

"Yes, *Ta-jen*," the shopkeeper said **glumly**. **"There is no question about that."**

"I am glad I was able to take care of this case," said the magistrate. "You have to watch out for these **troublemakers**. Next time, if you have a case like this, don't try to settle it yourself. Be sure to let me handle it for you."

....

glumly sadly
"There is no question about that." "That is true."
troublemakers people who cause trouble

BEFORE YOU MOVE ON...

1. **Evidence and Conclusions** The magistrate likes the farmer and wants to help him. What evidence supports this conclusion?

2. **Inference** The magistrate says he will handle situations like this in the future for the shopkeeper. Why does he say this?

Mr. Yeh's New Year

Some six hundred years ago, on New Year's Eve, Mr. Yeh was **on his way** home after being gone for almost a year. In his sack was a silver *yüan-pao*, the salary for a year's teaching in a private school some seventy *li* away. Mr. Yeh was very happy. He knew his wife would be waiting for him and for the money as well. She needed the money to buy food and wine for the New Year's Eve dinner.

No Chinese could afford to miss New Year's Eve dinner. It was the most important meal of the year, even more important than the dinner on New Year's Day. The Chinese always believed that a **well-provided**

on his way traveling
well-provided big, expensive

New Year's Eve dinner would **usher them smoothly into a prosperous** new year.

A typical New Year's Eve feast would include *ssu-ch'üan*, or four "wholes"—a whole chicken, a whole duck, a whole fish, and a whole leg of pork; four kinds of cold meat; *pa-pao-fan*, or "eight-treasure rice," a sweet rice dish with eight ingredients; and *pa-pao-ts'ai*, the "eight valuables," which is made of eight different kinds of vegetables and soybeans. If people could afford it, they would cook enough to last for the fifteen days of the New Year celebration. It not only showed that they were **well-off** enough to have food left over from the previous year, it also let them enjoy visiting with relatives and friends during the holidays without having to worry about cooking.

Mr. Yeh was quite sure that his wife had used up every penny she had and was "waiting for **rice to put into the pot**," as the saying goes. He wished he had wings so he could fly back home and give that silver *yüan-pao* to his wife right away. As he walked on, he started to plan the menu for the New Year's Eve dinner.

....

usher them smoothly into a prosperous bring them a successful

well-off rich, wealthy

rice to put into the pot her husband to bring her the money

He knew that they would probably not be able to buy four "wholes." But at least his wife could get some pork and cook his favorite, *hung-shao-jou*—pork stewed with red wine and red soybean sauce—which he would definitely **wash down** with his favorite rice wine . . .

What happened in the next few seconds was almost too sudden to describe. Mr. Yeh saw a woman run toward the river, just about to throw herself in. It was A-ken Sao, he realized, the wife of carpenter A-ken. He rushed to stop her, and **in a flash** A-ken Sao was caught in his arms.

"Let me go!" she cried. "Let me go!"

But Mr. Yeh would not let go. "A-ken Sao!" he said. "You mustn't end your life like this! What is the matter?"

"Let me die!" cried A-ken Sao. "I have not heard from A-ken for a whole year. He has either died or **abandoned** me. The rent on our land **is long overdue**, and now the landlord wants to sell my daughter, Ying-hua. I don't know what to do."

"Don't worry," said Mr. Yeh. "I am sure A-ken has just been delayed."

....

wash down eat together
in a flash quickly
abandoned left
is long overdue was not paid

"It can't be true. Since he left home a year ago, he has not written or even sent a message to me. I know he is dead! Oh, let me die!" cried A-ken Sao. But the more she struggled, the tighter Mr. Yeh held on.

"I am certain A-ken did write," said Mr. Yeh. He was **thinking hard for words**.

Suddenly A-ken Sao stopped struggling. "So you have a letter for me?"

Mr. Yeh let go of her and pretended to search his pockets. Then he smiled apologetically. "No, I don't have a letter."

"Oh!" cried A-ken Sao. She started for the river again.

"Don't, don't!" said Mr. Yeh. "A-ken didn't ask me to bring you a letter, but he sent you some money." He took out the precious silver *yüan-pao*, **rubbed it carefully on his robe**, and handed it to A-ken Sao.

A-ken Sao broke into a big smile as she took the *yüan-pao*. "Ying-hua is saved! Buddha protects us! Thank you, Mr. Yeh."

Mr. Yeh watched A-ken Sao hurry away. "**There goes** my New Year's Eve dinner!" he mumbled to

----

thinking hard for words trying to think of something nice to say

rubbed it carefully on his robe made it shine

There goes Now I will not have

himself. **With heavy steps**, he walked slowly toward home.

Sure enough, Mrs. Yeh was standing by the door when he arrived. "Old man, here you are! I was worried that something might have happened. You must be tired. I'll get you some water to wash your face."

After Mr. Yeh had washed his face and sat down at the table, Mrs. Yeh said, "Old man, **was this a good year for you**?"

"Oh, it was a good year. I earned a silver *yüan-pao*."

"**Thanks be to** Buddha! Now we can have a decent New Year's Eve dinner. Where is it?"

"Old woman, I don't have it anymore."

"What! What did you do with it?"

"I gave it to A-ken Sao. Her rent is overdue and she has not heard from A-ken for a whole year. She was about to drown herself."

"But what are we going to do? We don't have any food in the house. Couldn't you at least have saved part of it for us?"

"I told her that it was from A-ken. If I hadn't, she would not have taken it."

....

With heavy steps Sadly

was this a good year for you did you earn a lot of money this year

Thanks be to Praise

"But are we supposed to starve in the new year? We can't go to bed **with empty stomachs**. You will have to go and borrow some money."

So Mr. Yeh went out to borrow money. He knew that New Year's Eve was the worst time to do such a thing—not only because people were busy cooking dinner, but also because they believed that borrowers could bring them bad luck in the new year. Almost every **door was shut in Mr. Yeh's face**, and when a man finally handed him a small package, all he got was some dirt wrapped in a piece of paper.

Tired and disappointed, Mr. Yeh went home. "Let's go to bed and not think about dinner," he said to Mrs. Yeh.

"I am too hungry to sleep," said his wife. "Can't you do something?"

"What do you want me to do?"

"At least you can get us some sweet potatoes from the fields."

"Those sweet potatoes don't belong to us."

"Come over, let me **whisper into your ear**."

Mr. Yeh leaned over.

....

with empty stomachs without eating anything; hungry

door was shut in Mr. Yeh's face person refused to lend Mr. Yeh money

whisper into your ear tell you a secret

"What? You want me to steal?"

"**Shh, shh.** Don't use that word. Say 'move.'"

"That's the same thing. I am not going to do it."

"Old man, are you going to starve us to death?" Mrs. Yeh began to cry.

Finally, Mr. Yeh decided that he had to "move" some sweet potatoes into their home whether he liked it or not. So he took a basket and a knife and walked toward the fields.

The sweet-potato field belonged to a widow, Liu Sao, and her only son, young Hsiao-pao. Now, Liu Sao knew that New Year's Eve was usually a good time for people to steal sweet potatoes, since she would be busy cooking the New Year's dinner. This year, Liu Sao decided to **take extra precautions**. She walked her son to the fields to **stand guard** and promised to **relieve** him when she finished cooking dinner.

Hsiao-pao settled down in the tent his mother had pitched in the fields. He blew out the lamp and sat in the darkness. If somebody was going to come and steal, Hsiao-pao had to catch the thief by surprise. He had a heavy stick almost as tall as himself, which he would use

---

Shh, shh. Be quiet.

take extra precautions be extra careful

stand guard protect the potatoes

relieve guard for

to **strike the unwelcome visitor**. It would be a blow that no thief could ever forget.

After a long wait, during which he nearly fell asleep more than once, he saw a tall figure **creep surreptitiously** into the small chapel at the edge of the field, where the T'u-ti P'u-sa—the Buddha of earth—was worshipped. "I'd better go and take a look," he said to himself. Since he was used to walking in the dark, he got into the temple and hid behind the altar in no time.

A man was kneeling in front of the altar. In the dim candlelight, Hsiao-pao was surprised to see that it was his former teacher, Mr. Yeh.

Kowtowing incessantly to the statue of T'u-ti P'u-sa, Mr. Yeh said, "T'u-ti P'u-sa, T'u-ti P'u-sa, tell me what I am supposed to do. A-ken Sao almost killed herself because A-ken didn't come home, so I gave her my silver *yüan-pao*. Now my wife and I are going to starve. My wife wants me to 'move' some sweet potatoes from the fields—do you think it is all right for me to do so? If you think so, please show me **a sign**." Mr. Yeh stood up, picked up the *ch'ien* holder from the altar, drew out two *ch'ien,* and threw them on the

---

strike the unwelcome visitor hit the thief
creep surreptitiously walk secretly
Kowtowing incessantly to Humbly worshipping
a sign that you agree

ground. Then he closed his eyes and prayed.

Ch'ien are fortune-telling sticks people use to seek advice when they are not sure what to do. The *ch'ien* have long and short lines **engraved on** each side. The way to work the *ch'ien* is to throw two or three on the ground and read the pattern they form. A certain pattern will represent **a go-ahead sign**.

When Hsiao-pao heard what Mr. Yeh was praying about, he laughed silently. "Let me **play** T'u-ti P'u-sa," he said to himself. While Mr. Yeh's eyes were still closed, Hsiao-pao crawled under the altar and looked at the *ch'ien*. They did not form a go-ahead pattern. He quickly flipped one *ch'ien* over and crawled back under the altar.

Mr. Yeh opened his eyes, bent down, and looked at the *ch'ien*. They formed a go-ahead pattern. He smiled. "T'u-ti P'u-sa, you approved this. Thank you. But just to be sure, could you give me the sign one more time?" He threw two more *ch'ien* to the ground, closed his eyes, and prayed again.

Hsiao-pao, trying hard to keep from laughing aloud, crawled out to make sure that the *ch'ien* formed a

....

engraved on carved into
a go-ahead sign an agreement
play pretend to be

go-ahead pattern.

"Go-ahead again!" cried Mr. Yeh. "Oh, T'u-ti P'u-sa. Please give me the sign once more. As soon as I get some money, I will buy incense to honor you." He **worked** the *ch'ien* again, and, of course, he **was not disappointed**.

"Thank you, T'u-ti P'u-sa," said Mr. Yeh **reverently**. "I promise to pay Liu Sao and Hsiao-pao back as soon I find a way to get some money." Mr. Yeh kowtowed three times and walked out of the temple, with Hsiao-pao quietly following him.

"Ha, teacher," Hsiao-pao laughed to himself, "you always told us that one should never steal, but today, you yourself are **breaking the rule**." He stayed quietly on the edge of the field and watched as Mr. Yeh put down the basket he had brought with him and started to dig sweet potatoes with a knife.

Mr. Yeh was an excellent teacher but a terrible sweet-potato digger. He was so inexperienced and afraid of being discovered that he progressed very slowly. "T'u-ti P'u-sa," he cried again, "can't you give me some help?"

....

worked threw, tossed
was not disappointed saw the same pattern
reverently with great respect
breaking the rule stealing

Hsiao-pao almost burst out laughing. "Good, let's have some more fun," he said to himself. He took out a knife and started to dig up sweet potatoes from the plants around him with amazing speed. Then he tossed them at Mr. Yeh. Sweet potatoes **rained down** on the old teacher, and some of them hit **their target** right on his forehead.

"T'u-ti P'u-sa, thank you, thank you," cried Mr. Yeh, "but don't go too fast, I can't **keep up**!"

Figuring that Mr. Yeh had had enough, the "little T'u-ti P'u-sa" stopped. Mr. Yeh picked up his basket and went home.

Soon after, when Liu Sao went to the fields to relieve her son, she found him away from his tent. Many holes in the field had been dug, and a lot of sweet potatoes were missing.

"Hsiao-pao, where are you?" she cried.

"Shh, shh . . . Here I am." Hsiao-pao crept out from the dark. "I was playing T'u-ti P'u-sa."

"T'u-ti P'u-sa? Look, so many sweet potatoes are gone. You must have been sleeping!"

"No, Mr. Yeh stole them," said Hsiao-pao with a

---

rained down dropped
their target Mr. Yeh
keep up pick them up this quickly

mischievous smile.

"That's not a nice thing to say. Mr. Yeh is such a **decent old gentleman**."

"But it's true. And I helped him." Hsiao-pao told his mother the whole story.

"Poor Mr. Yeh. He must be having a hard time. Tomorrow morning let's go wish him a Happy New Year and take him some New Year food. He has always been so kind to you."

The next morning, Hsiao-pao and his mother went to wish Mr. Yeh and his wife a Happy New Year. As they were approaching the house, they were surprised to hear Mr. Yeh saying to Mrs. Yeh, "Old woman, **help yourself**, eat some *hung-shao-jou*," and Mrs. Yeh saying, "Old man, don't be shy, eat some cold sliced pork."

Hsiao-pao was very upset. "So Mr. Yeh was lying. If he has money to buy pork, why did he come to steal our sweet potatoes?"

"Shh, let's look," said his mother. They **peeped** through the window and saw Mr. Yeh putting a piece of red-skinned sweet potato into his wife's bowl as she was putting a white-skinned sweet potato into his bowl.

....

mischievous playful
decent old gentleman nice old man
help yourself take as much food as you want
peeped secretly looked; peeked

They were both **making believe** that they were eating pork!

Hsiao-pao laughed and banged on the door. "Mr. Yeh, Mr. Yeh!"

Mr. Yeh sprang from his chair and looked at his wife "Hsiao-pao is here!"

Mrs. Yeh quickly took away the remaining sweet potatoes, while Mr. Yeh looked for a place to hide the skins of the ones they'd eaten. He rushed over to the stove, threw the skins into a pot, and put the lid on.

Once in the house, Hsiao-pao knelt down and wished Mr. Yeh and his wife a Happy New Year. Mr. Yeh's face **became very red** when Liu Sao handed him the New Year food.

A minute later, A-ken Sao came in with her daughter, Ying-hua. "Thank you, Mr. Yeh, you saved us. Without the money you brought back to me, we would have **been lost**."

"So you are all here!" A voice behind them made them all turn around.

A-ken was standing by the door.

A-ken Sao was **ecstatic**. "A-ken, I came to thank

....

making believe pretending
became very red looked very embarrassed
been lost not been able to survive
ecstatic very happy

Mr. Yeh for bringing me the money you sent me. Without it, Ying-hua would have been sold."

"What is this all about?" asked A-ken. "I never asked Mr. Yeh to bring you any money." He looked confused.

"I know everything about this," said Hsiao-pao. And in a few sentences, he told the whole story.

A-ken and his wife **fell on their knees**. "Thank you, Mr. Yeh!" they said.

Hsiao-pao walked over to the stove. He took the lid off the pot where the sweet-potato skins were hidden. *"Hung-shao-jou!"* he exclaimed. Tossing them into the air, he laughed out loud.

....

fell on their knees were very thankful

BEFORE YOU MOVE ON...

1. **Cause and Effect** Why does Mr. Yeh finally agree to steal the sweet potatoes? Reread pages 67–68.

2. **Theme** What is the theme of this story?

The Miracle Doctor

About eighteen hundred years ago, there lived in China a doctor named Hua T'o. Using medicines he made from herbs, Hua T'o had saved thousands of people who were dying of **incurable diseases**. He was known as the "Miracle Doctor."

One hot and humid day, Hua T'o was traveling on the road and came across a man wailing beside a cart. Hua T'o walked up to the man, put his hand on his shoulder, and asked, "*Ta-ko*, what's the matter?"

"**I've been struck by disaster**," said the tearful man. "My daughter and I were on our way to visit some relatives when she suddenly became ill. There she is, lying in the cart. She is dead! I am sure she is dead!"

....

incurable diseases diseases that could not be healed
I've been struck by disaster Something terrible has happened

"Let me look at her," said Hua T'o. He gently lifted the cloth that covered the girl's face, and examined her eyes. Then he felt her pulse. "**Be of good cheer**," he said to the man. "Your daughter is not dead. I can **bring her back to consciousness**."

Hua T'o took **an acupuncture needle** from his sack, pushed it **deftly** into the girl's scalp, and drew it out immediately. Then he broke a branch from a tree, stuck it into the ground, and said to the man, "When the shadow of the stick becomes one *ch'ih* long, your daughter will awaken." He then gathered up his things and continued on his way.

The man sat on the side of the road and waited anxiously. When the shadow of the stick became one *ch'ih*, long, the girl opened her eyes.

"Where am I, Father?"

"My child, you almost died!" said the man. "Fortunately, a doctor came by and saved your life."

"A doctor? Where is he?" The girl's eyes followed her father's hand as he pointed to a small figure in the distance moving farther and farther away.

"It must be the Miracle Doctor!" she said.

....

Be of good cheer Do not worry
bring her back to consciousness wake her
an acupuncture needle a needle used to cure illnesses
deftly skillfully, carefully

A few days later, in a tavern on the side of a lonely road, Hua T'o was having a cup of tea. Two men sitting at a table in a corner were drinking heavily. One of them, who was in military uniform, took out a coin from his purse, tossed it on the table, and said to the tavern keeper, "Hey, fellow. Bring me another bottle of wine."

"I am sorry, sir," said the tavern keeper. "I am afraid that you have had too much to drink. Besides, I have only one bottle left, and I would like to save it for another customer."

"I'll drink and I'll pay," said the man. "But if you don't bring me the wine, you are not going to have a shop anymore."

The tavern keeper **paled**. Without another word, he brought the last bottle of wine over to the table.

The doctor saw everything. He picked up his walking stick, **strode** to the table where the two men were sitting, and, before the man in uniform had a chance to touch the bottle, he smashed it into pieces.

"Listen," he said to the man, "if you **cherish your life**, stay away from wine. You are seriously ill. If you

....

paled was scared
strode walked
cherish your life want to live

stop drinking, you may have three more months to live. If you continue to drink, you will be dead in three days." He picked up his sack and walked out of the tavern, leaving the two men stunned.

The man in military uniform seemed to have **sobered up a bit**. He rose and said to his companion, "Let's get out of here!"

As the two walked out, the man said, "This crazy old man said that I am sick. Do I look like someone who is sick? I am strong!" To prove what he said, he marched a few steps, but his legs shook and he **collapsed**.

Three months later, Hua T'o was on the road again. As he neared a small town, he saw a young girl running toward him. When she reached him, she fell on her knees and said, "Miracle Doctor, I am so glad I found you. I have been trying to find you so I could thank you for saving my life."

"Are you sure I saved your life, my child?" said the doctor. "I don't remember **treating** you at all."

"Of course you did!" said the girl. "My name is Lan Ying. Three months ago my father and I were going to

....

sobered up a bit become more serious
collapsed fell
treating helping

visit our relatives. I **fell** ill on the road and almost died. Luckily, you came by and saved my life. Surely you remember now?"

"Oh, now I do!" said Hua T'o. "I am so happy to see you well again. Where is your father, Lan Ying?"

"He is having a drink. Would you care to join us?" The girl pointed to a wine shop a few steps away.

"I would be glad to." The doctor followed the girl into the wine shop.

But as soon as he saw the girl's father, a strange look appeared on his face. "I am sorry, but I can't join you, *Ta-ko.* For your own good, stay away from wine." He quickly turned around and walked away.

The girl ran after him. "Doctor Hua, is there anything wrong?"

"Your father is seriously ill. He has a strange kind of disease that makes him **allergic to wine**. If he keeps on drinking, he will die very soon."

"Please do something!" cried Lan Ying. "You are the Miracle Doctor. You can treat any kind of disease!"

"I am very sorry," Hua T'o replied, shaking his head. "This is a deadly disease. So far, I have not found a cure

....

fell became

allergic to wine sick if he drinks wine

for it. Please forgive me." And **with a heavy heart** he went away.

Hua T'o's wife was anxiously waiting for him at home. "We are in trouble," she said. "There is a military man waiting for you in the living room. He refuses to leave until he sees you."

As the doctor walked into the living room, the man rose and bowed deeply. "Doctor Hua, I came to thank you for saving my life," he said. "Three months ago you caught me drunk in a tavern, **making a scene**. You told me that I **was terminally ill** and should stop drinking right away. I did not believe you, but then I collapsed right after you left. Fortunately, I sought treatment, and now I am cured. I came to thank you. Now I must go."

"Wait," said the doctor. "I did not know there was a cure for this kind of disease. Can you tell me who treated you?"

"I was lucky," the man replied. "The tavern keeper told me that on Mount Lotus a **monk** could treat this kind of disease. So I went up there, got five balls made from magic herbs, and was cured." He bowed and left.

....

with a heavy heart feeling sad
making a scene behaving badly
was terminally ill would die soon
monk religious man

That night Hua T'o could not sleep at all. The tearful face of Lan Ying kept appearing in his mind. "Hua T'o, Hua T'o!" he said to himself. "You are unworthy of the name Miracle Doctor. Hundreds of people are dying of this terrible disease, and you can do nothing to stop it. You must go up the mountain to find out about the magic cure."

But that was no easy task. The doctor knew all too well that the monk would never give the secret formula of his herb medicine to **an outsider**. Hua T'o would have to become a monk first. So he changed his name to Hsüeh Fang and traveled to Mount Lotus.

The temple where the monk lived was halfway up Mount Lotus. When the doctor reached it, he saw a long line of people waiting their turn to go in and see the monk. Many of them were carried either on the back of a relative or on a **stretcher**.

When it was the doctor's turn, he walked into the temple and went straight up to a monk who was sitting on a cushion in front of the altar with his legs folded under his body. The doctor knelt down and began to say aloud, "Teacher, my name is Hsüeh Fang, and I am

....

an outsider a stranger; someone who was not a monk
stretcher device used to carry sick people

a homeless man. I have decided to let go all worldly desires and become a monk. Please allow me to be one of your **disciples**."

The monk closed his eyes and said slowly, "Not everyone can **reach the height of holiness** and become a monk, Hsüeh Fang. I think we can use you only as a cleaning person. We will give you food and a place to sleep."

So the doctor became a cleaning person. Every day he swept the grounds outside the temple, hoping for a chance to find out about the magic cure. But it was a closely guarded secret. The monk even denied that he used herbs to treat patients. "I am a monk, not a doctor," he said to **his apprentices**. "I don't believe in medicine. I heal people with the supernatural power I gained from years of prayer and sacrifice. Only the pure and the **devout** will be given such power."

And yet every day, when the doctor was sweeping the grounds outside the temple, he noticed that after the patients had been seen by the monk, they would always leave the temple with five wax balls in their hands. The doctor knew that the secret was contained in those wax

....

disciples students
reach the height of holiness succeed
his apprentices the people he taught
devout faithful

balls. But whenever he asked a patient to let him look at them, the monk's oldest apprentice, Big Brother, would yell at him, "Don't stand there like that. Go back to work!" The doctor wasn't **making any progress**.

The monk had a younger apprentice, known as Little Brother, who was more friendly. Every morning he would climb up to the top of the mountain and collect herbs. Several times the doctor offered to go with him, but Little Brother would always say, "No. You can't come with me. Teacher does not want anyone to know the kind of herbs I collect for him."

The doctor knew there was a special room in the south **wing** of the temple, but no one except the monk and Big Brother was allowed to go there. Every night, after the apprentices and the doctor had gone to bed, the monk would lock himself in the room for hours.

One night, the doctor tried to find out what the monk was doing. Thinking that the two apprentices were in bed, he quietly made his way to the south wing. **From the shadow on the window paper** he could see that the monk was stirring something in a pot on a stove. He smelled herbs but could not tell exactly what

....

making any progress learning anything about the secret wax balls

wing side

From the shadow on the window paper Through the window

they were. As he stood there, he felt a hand grabbing his shoulder. It was Big Brother's.

"What are you doing, Hsüeh Fang?" Big Brother demanded. "How dare you come here! Go back to bed!"

Without **uttering** a word, the doctor obeyed.

A month passed. Hua T'o had still not learned the secret of the magic cure. But one day an opportunity came.

The monk **happened to be** out for a visit, and his two apprentices were seeing patients inside the temple. As the doctor was sweeping the ground outside, he was surprised to see Lan Ying coming out of the temple with five wax balls in her hand. Behind her **trudged** a man carrying her father on his back. The doctor went up to Lan Ying and drew her aside.

"Lan Ying," he said softly.

Lan Ying was surprised. "What are you doing here, Doctor Hua?"

"**Hush**, don't call me Doctor," he said in a low voice. "People here know me only as a cleaning person. I came to find out the secret of the magic cure. I need

....

uttering saying
happened to be was
trudged walked
Hush Quiet

your help. Please lend me one of the wax balls you have in your hand. I want to find out the ingredients in the medicine. Then I can make one exactly like this and return it to you."

Lan Ying hesitated. "I can't take the risk," she said. "Big Brother said that my father needs to take one ball a day for five **consecutive days**. If he misses one, he will die."

"My child," Lan Ying's father called. He had also recognized the doctor. "You can't say no to Doctor Hua. He saved your life. I trust him."

Slowly, the girl handed the doctor one of the wax balls. "Take it, Doctor. But please remember that my **father's life depends on your returning it on time**."

"I promise you I will make one exactly the same as this and bring it to you on the fifth day," said Hua T'o. "Where are you staying?"

"We will be staying at **an inn near the foot** of the mountain."

"I will find you there," said the doctor.

The doctor ran back into his room and shut the

----

consecutive days days in order; days in a row

father's life depends on your returning it on time father will die if you do not return the ball to me on the fifth day

an inn near the foot a place near the bottom

door. He peeled off the wax and **dissolved** the herb ball in water. He dipped his finger in the mixture and tasted it.

"How strange! His formula is exactly the same as mine. We have been using the same kinds of herbs to treat that deadly disease, but why is it that my medicine doesn't work? Is it because the yellow flowers that grow on this mountain are more powerful than the ones I use?"

Suddenly the door flew open and Big Brother walked in. He **snatched** the bowl from the doctor's hands and looked at it. "So you came to steal the formula, you thief!" he cried. "Get out!" He spilled the medicine on the ground.

The doctor had no choice but to pick up his things and leave.

Little Brother, who had now become his friend, followed him sadly. Handing him a bunch of yellow flowers, he said, "Brother Hsüeh, I am so sorry to see you go. Here are some herbs I gathered this morning. Take them with you. You may need them."

The doctor thanked him and started to walk down

....

dissolved mixed
snatched angrily took

the mountain. Just then he heard loud cries coming from the temple.

"Big Brother is **possessed by the devil** again," said Little Brother. "Don't worry about him. You'd better be on your way before Teacher gets back."

But Hua T'o rushed back into the temple. He saw Big Brother rolling on the floor, moaning. He checked the man's eyes, **felt his pulse, and then pressed his abdomen**. He could tell that the man was seriously ill and would die if he did not have **surgery** at once. But should he do it? He might not have time to get away before the monk came back.

"Get me some wine," he told Little Brother, who came in after him. Hua T'o took a paper package from his sack and poured the contents into the bowl of wine that Little Brother brought him. "Go out and keep a watch for Teacher. If you see him coming, cough loudly."

Hua T'o pried open Big Brother's mouth with a chopstick and forced the medicine down his throat. The man became still. The doctor took out a small knife and started to operate on the man's abdomen. Just when he

....

possessed by the devil sick

felt his pulse, and then pressed his abdomen and then examined him for signs of illness

surgery an operation

finished the surgery he heard Little Brother coughing.

Hua T'o quickly covered the **incision** with a clean cloth, gathered his things and the bunch of yellow flowers, and hurried out of the temple, only to find himself face-to-face with the monk.

The monk looked at the yellow flowers in the doctor's hands. He snatched them away and said, "So I was right. I have always suspected that you were a **quack** doctor. And you came here to steal my secret formula."

"Yes, I am a doctor," said Hua T'o. "Are you not one? Are you not treating patients with herbal medicine just as we doctors do? Why do you refuse to share your secret when you want to save lives?"

The monk looked angry. "Leave at once," he ordered.

Disheartened, the doctor started down the mountain.

In the meantime, the monk walked into the temple and saw his big apprentice lying on the floor with a cloth covering his abdomen.

"Look," said Little Brother, "Big Brother has opened

....

incision cut from the operation
quack crazy, fake
Disheartened Disappointed

his eyes."

The monk took off the cloth and examined the incision. It was made perfectly. Only the hands of the most skillful doctor could have done that. He then picked up the bowl from the table, dipped his finger into the medicine, and tasted it.

"*Ma-fei-san!* This is the special kind of **anesthetic** the Miracle Doctor Hua T'o uses in surgery. And yet Hsüeh Fang used it to save my apprentice's life! He must be the Miracle Doctor!"

Hua T'o was moving slowly down the mountain. "I have failed," he said to himself. Without the yellow flowers, he could not **reproduce** the medicine. What was he going to tell Lan Ying and her father when he saw them? How could he tell them that Lan Ying's father was going to die?

"Brother Hsüeh Fang! Brother Hsüeh Fang!" Little Brother called, running after him. In his hands he was holding a bag. "Teacher told me to give this to you."

The doctor opened the bag and found a note inside. It read: "Blossoming yellow flowers in March, useless weeds in April." What did that mean? He put his hand

---

anesthetic medicine
reproduce make

in the bag and took out a bunch of dried yellow flowers.

All of a sudden he knew! The secret was simple! The reason his medicine didn't work was because he had always used fresh yellow flowers collected in April, when they were fully grown. The medicine had by then **spread** into the leaves and no longer remained in the roots. The monk was telling him that to cure the strange disease he should use the dried roots of the yellow flowers that grew in March instead, because that was where the medicine **was stored**! The note in his hand held the secret of the cure for the deadly disease! **He could hardly believe it.**

The Miracle Doctor followed the monk's instructions and made the medicine. He saved many people from that strange disease. And the first one he saved, of course, was Lan Ying's father.

....

spread gone
was stored could be found; was kept
He could hardly believe it. He was surprised.

BEFORE YOU MOVE ON...

1. **Character's Motive** Why does Hua T'o the Miracle Doctor want the monk's secret medicine?

2. **Inference** Reread page 92. The monk sends the recipe for his medicine to Hua T'o as a riddle. Why?

The Royal Bridegroom

It was close to midnight. In the wedding chamber of the Royal Palace, Princess Yün-hua, sitting by the side of her bed, **let forth** a deep sigh. She had been there since the wedding ceremony, and the red silk **veil** covering her head was making her very uncomfortable. Although she could not see anybody through the veil, she knew that her *kung-o*—her **maids-in-waiting—had already withdrawn to their quarters** and she was alone with the bridegroom, her *fu-ma*.

The princess was glad at least that the wedding ceremony was over. It had been such a long one, and since her head was covered by the veil the whole time, she had to do everything with the help of her *kung-o*, as

---

let forth breathed

veil cloth

maids-in-waiting—had already withdrawn to their quarters servants—had already gone to bed though **she were blindfolded**. She never even got a chance to see her *fu-ma*'s face and wondered if he was as attractive as the emperor, her brother, had said. Anyway, she knew she was going to find out soon.

As she sat there, she heard a deep sigh. Fu-ma must be tired, too. She lifted her veil and peeped out. Fu-ma had risen from the place where he had been sitting and was **pacing** back and forth across the room. Then he turned around, and she saw his face. How handsome he was! So her brother, the emperor, was right! But why didn't Fu-ma come to take off her veil? It was time for them to have their **private toast**. What was bothering him?

Finally, the princess could not wait any longer. She decided to break the rules and take off the veil herself. Putting it aside, she called out to her *fu-ma*, who, for some reason, had stopped pacing. He was sitting down on a chair.

"Fu-ma, this is our wedding night. Let's have a toast," the princess said gently.

"Serve the wine," Fu-ma ordered **arrogantly**.

The princess was shocked. She had never expected

....

she were blindfolded her eyes were covered
pacing walking
private toast special wedding drink
arrogantly rudely

Fu-ma to be so rude. Nevertheless, she filled a cup with wine and brought it over to Fu-ma, who gulped it down.

"Another cup," he ordered.

The princess was **perplexed**. How dare he behave like this? But she didn't want a quarrel on her wedding night, so she **suppressed her resentment**, filled the cup a second time, and handed it to Fu-ma. Again, Fu-ma drank it off without waiting for a toast.

"Fill up the cup," he ordered for a third time.

The princess could control her anger no longer. She put the wine pitcher down on the table. "Fu-ma, how dare you order me about like a servant. Please remember that I am a princess."

"But now you have become my wife. You should follow my rules," said Fu-ma without even looking at her.

"Your rules?" The princess was **astounded**.

"Yes. My rules. Every morning you should get up before I do. Lay out my clothes and my shoes. Make sure my tea is made properly and my meals are well cooked."

....

perplexed confused and angry
suppressed her resentment hid her anger
astounded surprised and angry

"I have never done those things before!" cried the princess.

"It's high time you learned," Fu-ma continued. "And that is not all. You must give me a son within a year. If you don't, I will divorce you."

"Divorce me? You wouldn't dare!" The princess was outraged.

"Why not? This is **the law of heaven and earth**. If you fail to give birth to a son, you will be divorced."

"What if I have a daughter?"

"A daughter? If you give birth to a daughter, you will be asked to take your own life. Your job is to produce **an heir**. If you fail to do so, you shall die. That will save you from disgrace."

"Let's see if you dare ask me to do such a thing! I am going to talk to my brother right now; he will have your head cut off!" the princess **retorted vehemently**. She stood up and was about to summon her maids to accompany her to see the emperor.

"Not so fast!" said Fu-ma. He threw back his head and laughed. "I was only joking. All I wanted was to show you the kind of life ordinary women live. You

....

the law of heaven and earth the way it has always been
an heir a son who will replace me as prince someday
retorted vehemently answered angrily

are a princess. You have always been **waited upon hand and foot**, so you have no sympathy for ordinary women at all."

"How do you know?" asked the princess. She felt insulted.

"Well, I can prove that later. But, first, let me tell you a story." Fu-ma suddenly seemed to be **in good humor**.

"There was once a high official who wanted a son so badly, he warned his wife that she would be asked to take her life if she gave birth to a daughter. The woman was terrified. When she did give birth to a girl, she wrote to her husband in the capital and told him she had given birth to a boy. The official was delighted. The girl was dressed like a boy and **brought up** as a boy. She learned to read and write and proved to be just as intelligent as any boy could be. At the age of eighteen, she was summoned by her father to the capital to take the imperial examinations. She did so well that she was selected by the emperor himself to be the *chuang-yüan* of the year."

"Unbelievable!" the princess exclaimed.

....

waited upon hand and foot cared for by others
in good humor in a good mood; cheerful
brought up was raised

"But soon trouble began. High officials in the imperial court began to propose marriage **on behalf of** their daughters. She turned down all the proposals. But when the emperor issued a royal **decree granting her the hand of** the daughter of one of his highest officials, she knew she could no longer refuse, or she would be punished."

"Then what did she do?" asked the princess.

"She had to obey the decree and go through the wedding ceremony. Can you imagine how she felt afterward, when she was left alone for the first time in the wedding chamber with her bride? On the other hand, what would you have done if you were that high official's daughter and discovered on your wedding night that your bridegroom was in fact a woman?"

"I don't believe that really happened," said the princess. "If it did happen, though, I would forgive that woman and ask my father, the high official, to beg the emperor to **pardon** the woman for disguising herself as a man."

"Do you really mean it?" asked Fu-ma.

"Of course I do. I am a princess. I always mean what

---

on behalf of for

decree granting her the hand of order saying she must marry

pardon excuse; not punish

I say."

Fu-ma let out a sigh of relief as he dropped to his knees. "Princess, I am that woman!"

"No," cried the princess. "This can't be true!"

"Why not?" asked Fu-ma.

"Because if you are a woman, then I don't have a husband anymore. If you are a woman, I am going to kill you!" The princess reached for a **sword** that was hanging on the wall.

"Princess, you said that you would forgive the woman and ask the emperor to grant her pardon."

"Yes, I said that because I didn't know you were that woman," the princess said angrily.

"You said you always meant what you said," Fu-ma reminded her.

"I said that because I didn't know you were that woman."

"Princess, don't you have any sympathy for an ordinary woman?" said Fu-ma sadly.

"Ordinary woman! Ordinary woman! Does an ordinary woman have a wedding night like this?" The princess was almost **in tears**. "Even if I can forgive

....

sword sharp weapon
in tears crying

you," she continued, "my brother, the emperor, will not. Don't you know that it is a **mortal offense** for a woman to disguise herself as a man and set foot in the palace? You have cheated the emperor, and this is a crime that cannot be pardoned. Once your true identity is revealed, **it will become a scandal** in the palace, and you will be put to death in no time."

"Princess, please let me go," pleaded Fu-ma.

"Go? Where can you go? The palace is strictly guarded, and nobody can leave at night. Tomorrow we are expected to appear as a newlywed couple in front of the emperor and greet the **well-wishers**. If you depart without an explanation, my brother will feel so insulted that I am sure he will issue an imperial decree to have you arrested. No matter where you go, you will be found. There is no place for you to hide. I can't pretend all my life that I am married to you; I don't want to kill you; I can't keep you here. Oh! What am I going to do with you?" The princess burst into tears.

A **faint** smile appeared on Fu-ma's face. "Princess, there is a way," she said calmly.

"What is it?" asked the princess as she took out a red

---

mortal offense crime that is punished by death
it will become a scandal everyone will be talking about it
well-wishers guests who want to congratulate us
faint small

silk handkerchief to wipe away her tears.

"Don't you know the saying 'cook it the same way'?" asked Fu-ma.

"'Cook it the same way'?" the princess repeated.

"Yes. When I told you the story about that woman, it was easy for you to forgive her because you didn't know you were also part of the story. If we 'cook it the same way' and tell the emperor the same story, maybe he will pardon me."

"That's a wonderful idea!" cried the princess. "And I guess I know how to tell it to make sure he will **be moved**. I think that you are very clever. I wish you really were my husband! What a pity! Well, now I think it is time for bed. I am quite tired." The two blew out the candles and **retired for the night**.

The next morning, the emperor summoned all his high officials to the palace. He wanted to introduce his sister and her new husband to them.

"The Princess *Ch'ien-sui* and Fu-ma!" announced a man.

The princess, dressed in a beautiful long pink dress, walked in with her husband, who was wearing a robe

....

be moved feel sad for the poor couple
retired for the night went to sleep

of a similar color. Fu-ma's father smiled proudly at his "son," who ignored him. The princess and Fu-ma went down on their knees and **wished the emperor good health**.

"Rise, my dear sister and Fu-ma," said the emperor. He was delighted, thinking that he had found the perfect husband for his sister. "Did you sleep well?"

"In fact, we spent the whole night talking," said the princess. "Fu-ma told me the most incredible story I have ever heard."

"That's wonderful. Be seated, my dear sister, and you, too, Fu-ma. Let's all hear the story."

"A girl was brought up as a boy because her father did not want a daughter," the princess began. "Her identity was kept a secret from the moment she was born. She learned everything a boy would learn, and she was as intelligent as any boy could be."

"That is hard to believe!" said the emperor, listening with interest.

"Well, when she was eighteen, her father, an official in the imperial court, told her to go to the capital and take the imperial examinations. She

....

wished the emperor good health honored the emperor

finished with flying colors and was selected by the emperor to be *chuang-yüan*. Besides this, the emperor gave the daughter of his defense minister to her in marriage."

"What a fool that emperor was!" exclaimed the princess's brother. "I cannot imagine how he could have failed to **distinguish** a woman from a man. How did the story end?"

"Well, when the woman's identity was finally revealed, the emperor felt that since he was the one who had made the mistake, he should be responsible for it. So he pardoned the woman. But he did more than that. He was so impressed by her talent, he **adopted her** as his sister."

"That's a delightful story," said the emperor. "I love the happy ending."

"Would *Wan-sui* do the same if it really happened to you?" asked the princess.

"Of course. Why not?" the emperor said, without thinking.

Fu-ma dropped to her knees. "I thank *Wan-sui* for his mercy!"

....

finished with flying colors did well on all of her tests
distinguish see, recognize
adopted her welcomed her into his family

The emperor was astounded. "What does this mean?" he demanded.

"I am a woman," said Fu-ma.

The emperor flew into a rage. "How dare you cheat your emperor! How dare you set foot on the **sacred** steps of the imperial palace. Guards, take her out and **behead her**!"

The imperial guards rushed over and were about to **lay their hands on** the woman. But there was a loud cry in the court: Fu-ma's father had fainted.

Fu-ma stood up. "An emperor never **plays with his words**. *Wan-sui* has already granted me pardon, and he cannot go back on his word."

"That's right," said the princess. "Also, if Fu-ma is beheaded, I will become a widow, since legally we are still married."

The whole court became very quiet. Everyone was waiting for the emperor to say something.

Finally, after a period of silence, the emperor let out a laugh. "I didn't realize that I was making a fool of myself. You are right, my dear sister. I am responsible for all this. Well, I guess I have no choice but to do

....

sacred holy, special
behead her cut off her head; kill her
lay their hands on grab, take
plays with his words lies

what was done in the story. Yes, I will pardon Fu-ma and make her my sister. As for you, my dear sister, the marriage will be **annulled**, and I will find another fine young man to be your husband."

"Thank you, *Wan-sui*!" cried the princess and Fu-ma as they went down on their knees again.

So Fu-ma became the emperor's adopted sister. A week later, the two princesses were married to two **fine** young officials in a joint wedding ceremony **presided over** by the emperor himself.

....

annulled cancelled
fine nice
presided over led

BEFORE YOU MOVE ON...

1. **Conclusions** What would have happened if Fu-ma's father had known she was a girl? Reread page 98.

2. **Paraphrase** Reread page 103. What does Fu-ma mean by "cook it the same way"? Why does this method work so well?

Pronunciation Guide

Note: I have chosen the Wade-Giles system to romanize Chinese names and terms. In the Wade-Giles system, an apostrophe is used to indicate when certain consonants are to be aspirated: for instance, *Ch'in* is pronounced "chin" while *Chin* is "jin." Also, in Wade-Giles, *ü* indicates a sound like the letter "u" in French.

A-ken Sao: ah-ghen sao
Chang Chen: jang jen
Chang T'ien-shih: jang tien-sh ("sh" prolonged)
Chao: jao
Chekiang: juh-jiang
Ch'i: chee
ch'ien: chien

Ch'ien-sui: chien-sway

ch'ih: ch (prolonged)

ch'i-lin: chee-lin

Chin: jin

Ch'in: chin

Ching: jing

Ch'ing: ching

Ch'u: choo

chuang-yüan: jwang-yüan

Chui-yü: jwai-yü

Feng Meng-lung: fung meng-loong

fu-ma: foo-mah

Han: han

Ho-shih: huh-sh ("sh" prolonged)

Hsia hsiu-ts'ai kuo-nien: shia shiou-tsai gwoh-nien

Hsiang-ling: shiang-ling

Hsiao-pao: shiau-bao

Hsi-ch'ü: shee-chü

Hsüeh Fang: shüeh fahng

Hsüeh Hsiang-ling: shüeh shiang-ling

hua-chiao: hwah-jiau

hua-pen: hwah-bun

Hua T'o: hwah twuh

hung-shao-jou: hoong-shao-roe
Kiangsu: jiang-soo
Kuan Han-ch'ing: gwan han-ching
Kuan-yin: gwan-yin
kung-o: goong-uh
Lai-chou: lie-joe
Lan Ying: lan ying
Lao-yeh: lau-yeh
li: lee
Li: lee
liang: liang
Lin Hsiang-ju: lin shiang-roo
Liu Sao: lyou sao
Lo Kuan-chung: luo gwan-joong
Lu: loo
ma-fei-san: mah-fay-san
Miao Hsien: miau shien
Mu: moo
Nü-chung-lang: nü-joong-lang
Pao Ch'eng: bao cheng
Pao Kung: bao goong
pa-pao-fan: bah-bao-fan
pa-pao-ts'ai: bah-bao-tsai

Pien Ho: bien huh
Pien-liang: bien–liang
San-kuo yen-i: san-gwoh yen-yi
Sao: sao
Shanghai: shang–hai
Shao-hsing-hsi: shao–shing–shee
Shui-hu: shway–hoo
So-lin-nang: swoh–lin–nang
ssu-ch'üan: ss–chüan ("ss" prolonged)
Sung: soong
ta-hsi-jih-tzu: dah-shee-rur-dz ("dz" prolonged)
Ta-jen: dah–run
Ta-ko: dah–guh
T'ang: tang
Ta-wang: dah–wang
Teng-chou: dung–joe
Tung-chou lieh-kuo chih: doong–joe lieh–gwoh jh
   ("jh" prolonged)
T'u-ti P'u-sa: too–dee poo–sah
Wan-sui: wan–sway
Wei: way
Wei Jan: way ran
Wen: wen

Wu: woo
wu-kung: woo–goong
Yeh: yeh
Yen: yen
Ying-hua: ying–hwah
Yüan: yüan
Yüan-hsiao: yüan–shiau
yüan-pao: yüan–bao
Yüan-wai: yüan–why
Yün-hua: yün–hwah
Yu-yang: yo–yahng

Glossary

Chang T'ien-shih: a deity known for his ability to expel demons and spirits

ch'ien: fortune-telling sticks made of bamboo or wood

Ch'ien-sui: a term used to address members of an emperor's family, equivalent to "Your Royal Highness"

ch'ih: a unit of Chinese measurement that equals about thirteen inches

chuang-yüan: the first-place winner of the imperial examinations

fu-ma: the husband of a princess; also used as an address

imperial examinations: examinations to select young men to become high officials

Jade Emperor: a powerful deity who rules the heavens

kowtow: a body gesture—usually kneeling and then touching the ground with one's forehead—that shows one's submissive reverence. According to the Wade-Giles system, the word should be spelled "k'o-t'ou"; however, since it has been widely accepted in the West as "kowtow," I have decided to retain this form.

Kuan-yin: a compassionate Buddha who is considered the savior of the poor and the suffering

Lao-yeh: respectful form of address to a man who is wealthy or is a high official

li: a unit of length that equals five hundred meters

liang: a unit of weight for precious metals that equals approximately one ounce *ma-fei-san*: a special kind of anesthetic invented by Hua T'o (?–208)

Sao: literally means "sister-in-law," but is also used to address married women in the neighborhood

Ta-jen: a term a commoner used to address an official

Ta-ko: literally, "big brother"; often used to address a man whom one did not know personally

Ta-wang: a term used by a subject to address the king, equivalent to "Your Majesty"

Wan-sui: literally, "ten thousand years" (long life); a term used to address the emperor exclusively, equivalent to "Your Majesty"

Warring States (475–221 B.C.): an important period in Chinese history, during which the kings of several states under the reign of the sovereigns of the Chou Dynasty made war on one another

Yüan-hsiao Festival: the fifteenth day of the new year and the last day of the New Year celebration *yüan-pao*: a bar of precious metal, usually made of gold or silver

Yüan-wai: esquire, gentleman, sometimes used as part of a name, such as in "The Ch'i-lin Purse"

Author's Acknowledgments

I want to thank my father, Joseph Fang, for guiding me tirelessly through my research on the original Chinese texts. Also, I wish to express my profound gratitude to my friends Laurence Yep, Pat Markun, and Robin Moore; to my former English professor John Hirsh, who encouraged me to write the book; to my friend Jeanne Casey and my sister Helen, who edited the first few drafts of my manuscript; to my niece Elizabeth Rose, who assisted me in romanizing the Chinese names and place-names; and, last but not least, to my editor, Wes Adams, whose insightful queries inspired me to go back into the treasure house to search for more treasures, to Jeanne M. Lee for her beautiful artwork, and to my agent, Barrie Van Dyck, whose advice played a crucial role in this project.